To:

From:

To my biggest supporters of whatever I do in life, a.k.a

The Knebel Team!

SPELLING PEN

IN ELF LAND

Book #1

by C. Knebel
Simple Words Books™

FREE DECODABLE
PHONICS WORKBOOK
and
FREE ACCESS TO
ONLINE PARENTS' SUMMITS

simplewordsbooks.com

Chapter 1

Matt's Big Day

Matt springs out of bed. It is a big day for him. At last, he is ten!

He slips into his pants and top. He can smell brunch. He runs down the steps and past the hall with a yell.

"Yum!" he says. "Is that ham and eggs for me?"

His mom stands with a pan in her hand. She sets it down and hugs Matt. "Yes, this is for you. Grab a dish."

"Thanks, Mom!" Matt says.

"My son is getting so big!" says Matt's dad as he brings Matt a glass of milk.

"I want to get big quick as well," says Liz.

Matt and Liz are siblings. Liz is six. She is fond of Matt and wants to be just like him.

Matt spots a stack of gifts in the den. He wants to dig into them.

"Not yet!" his mom says. "Finish your eggs and ham. Then you can get to the gifts."

Matt gulps down his brunch. He sets his dish and cup in the sink.

Then he asks, "Can I go get my gifts?"

"Yes, Son," his dad nods.

They all run into the den.

"Pick this gift," says Liz. She hands Matt a big box with a red string. "It is from Mom, Dad and me."

Matt rips into the box. It is a big black tank and a bag of blocks.

"This tank was at the top of my wish list!" he yells with a thrill. "Thanks, Mom! Dad! Liz!" He hugs all of them.

Matt gets lots of gifts. He unpacks all of them.

The last gift is a box from Grandma Deb. Matt thinks it will be the best gift yet. So he has kept her gift for last. Grandma Deb is rich. Plus, she sticks to the kids' wish lists.

"Best for last," Matt rips the box.

"What is in the box?" asks Liz. "What did Grandma Deb get for you? Is it a big black jet? An i-pad? Tell me, Matt!"

"Oh, it is... just a pen with a glass pot of ink," he grunts.

This cannot be all of it. Matt checks the box. But there is not a thing left in it.

"Why did she get you a pen?" asks Liz. "What is up with Grandma Deb? Did you not send her your wish list for the gifts? Do not tell me that a pen was on your list."

"Not at all," says Matt. "Why did she get me a gift this bad?"

"There are no bad gifts," says his mom. She picks up the pen. "This is an old pen. It must have cost her a lot."

Matt is sad. He did not want a pen. But he stops to fuss.

"Well, I have got lots of things to play with," he thinks.

He flings the pen down and forgets it.

Chapter 2

The Gift

Matt likes most of his gifts. He thinks the tank and the blocks are the best.

Liz and Matt go out in the back to play with the tank. Liz helps Matt set up a big wall of blocks for the tank to blast.

They spend most of the day in the sun. They like to play on the grass. It is a lot of fun.

"Matt, you must thank Grandma Deb for the gift," his mom calls from the steps. "Get in and jot a quick thank you with the pen you got from her," she adds.

"Do I have to, Mom?" he asks.

"Yes, Matt. You must," his mom nods.

"I will when I get in," says Matt.

"Just do it, Matt," his mom says. "Then you can go out and play with the tank and the blocks. I left the pen and the ink on your desk."

"O.K.," Matt grunts as he gets up.

"I will set up the wall of blocks for the next blast," says Liz.

Matt does not say a thing back to Liz as he runs in.

Matt cannot spell well. Plus, his penmanship is bad. The kids in Matt's class think he is a slug. But he is not. He does his best. Yet, he just does not do as well as the rest.

Not like Liz. Liz is just six. Yet she can spell as well as Matt can. She is the best in all she does.

Matt gets sad and upset when he thinks of this. And he does not want to think of pens or spelling. He just wants to be out in the sun with Liz.

The pen and the ink pot are on his desk. Matt picks up the pen. The pen has a tag with a big sun on it. He rips the tag off and drops the tag in the trash bin.

He dips the pen in the black ink. He fills the pen with the ink.

A drop of ink drips on Matt's desk. The ink drop glints for a sec. But Matt does miss that.

Then he gets a pad and thinks of what to say. He must think of things he can spell, but what can that be?

"I wish I was not so bad at spelling," he thinks.

His mom will help if he asks. So will Liz. But he does not want to ask.

He jots: "I wish... I wish I just vanish..."

He does not get to finish it all. But he thinks it with all his will.

Just then, Liz steps in. "The wall of blocks is up, Matt," she says. Then she yells in shock, "What is that!"

"What?" Matt asks.

"The pen!" Liz yells. "Check the pen!"

The pen glints in Matt's hand. Then it emits a flash.

Matt sticks the pen in his pocket fast to stop the glinting pen. But that does not help.

A thick fog fills in. It gets dim. Liz grabs Matt's hand. Bit by bit, things swing and then spin. Liz and Matt spin as well. They spin fast. Then it all stops. And the kids drop down like a rock.

Chapter 3

In Elf Land

At last, there is no spinning. All is still. But what is this? There are no walls. No rug. No bed. Where can they be?

Matt sits up. They are next to a path in a big thicket.

"Liz, are you O.K.?" he asks.

"Where are we?" she gasps.

"I cannot tell," Matt says as he stands up. Then he helps Liz get up as well.

"How did we get to this land?" Liz asks. "And how will we get back?"

"I think it was this pen," Matt says.

"But Matt..." Liz is on the brink of sobbing.

Just then, quick steps thud on the path.

"Shh!" says Matt.

He rests his hand on Liz's.

The kids check who it is.

A small kid is rushing down the path. He is in a red outfit with a red cap. As he runs to them, they spot that this is not a kid like them.

"It is an elf!" Matt yells.

His yells ring in the thicket. The elf kid spots Matt and Liz.

"It is you at last! You are in our land!" he gasps. He runs back up the path.

"That was odd," says Matt.

"What was that? Shall we run?" Liz asks in a panic.

As they think of where to go, thudding steps fill the thicket. The elf kid runs in front of a big gang.

"There they are!" the elf kid sings. He gets his cap off and grins.

Liz steps next to Matt. She grabs his hand.

A tall elf steps in front of the kids.

"The Sun Kids!" he says. "The Sun Kids are in our land! You bring us luck.

We in Elf Land are so glad!"

"The Sun Kids?" Liz says to Matt. "Who are the Sun Kids? Who are you?"

"I am Twigs," says the tall elf. "And this is our elf clan."

"Well, Twigs," Matt says. "Do you think we are the Sun Kids?"

The elf clan nods.

"But we are not," Matt insists. "I can tell you that. I think there is a big mix up. So if you just let us go..."

"I am Mell." An elf in black steps up. "Then what shall we call you?" he asks.

"I am Matt," he says.

Liz stands still. She gets a pinch from Matt. "And I am Liz," she jumps in. "We are not the Sun Kids. Just lost kids! Where are we?"

"Matt and Liz, this is Elf Land," says Twigs. "I think you are the Sun Kids! All in this land are told of them. They will help Elf Land on a big quest."

"Yes, that is so!" yells an elf in the back.

"And Elf Land is at risk," adds Mell.

"Plus, you got the Spelling Pen," says Twigs. "You must be the Sun Kids."

Chapter 4

Elf Land At Risk

"The Spelling Pen?" Matt asks. "What is that?"

"It is sticking out of your pocket," says Twigs.

Matt brings the pen he got from Grandma Deb out of his pocket. It does not glint or flash.

"The Spelling Pen is the gift that will help us win the quest," Twigs adds. "And you must tell us your big plan to help Elf Land. But we cannot stand on this path for long. We must go."

"Plan? What plan? I have no plan!" insists Matt in shock.

But the elf clan is in a rush. They shush the kids and run with them down the path. They all run until they get to a bunch of huts.

Mell, Twigs and the kids cram into Mell's hut. The rest of the elf clan are off to their huts and to do their jobs.

"Sit on the bench, Sun Kids. Can I get you a drink or a snack?" asks Twigs.

Liz says yes to a drink, but Matt says no.

"I still do not get it," Matt says. "The Sun Kids? The Spelling Pen? What is all this?"

Twigs hands Liz a mug. She sips her hot drink.

"Yum!" she says. "It is like plums."

But Matt cannot think of plum drinks.

"You must tell us all there is," says Matt. "The Sun Kids and the Spelling Pen. Not a thing left out."

Twigs and Mell sit on a log next to the bench.

"In the past, Elf Land was a land of bliss, not just for the elf clan but for all. Rabbits, imps, griffins and goblins," Twigs says.

"Goblins?" yells Liz.

"Griffins and imps?" Matt gasps.

"Yes," says Twigs. "Well, the griffins have left Elf Land. Are there no goblins, griffins or imps in the land where you are from?"

"No," Liz grins. "I have yet to spot a griffin or goblin."

"That is odd," Mell says. "What a dull land it must be with no goblins or griffins. But be glad that you do not have imps. They are just bad."

"Go on," says Matt. "Where are the griffins?" asks Liz.

"They are in Obelisk Land," says Twigs. "We can go there as well. But this is our land."

"This was a glad land in the past. Goblins and imps did not mess with us. They did not bug us. And we let them be. But then, he got selfish and smug."

"He?" Matt jumps in. "Who is he?"

Twigs stops to rest. Then he adds, "He is King Gris. He was a grand elf. He was a rich elf king. Yet, he was not glad with his big stack of gold. He dug for gold. And he cut down the plants to melt the gold in his big kiln."

"Why did the griffins go?"

"He dug and dug until no plants were left in the West of Elf Land," Mell tells the kids. "Then, he went to Ash Hill to kill all the plants. That is when the griffins left."

"His next plan is for a big dig up on Drum Hill where we are. This is the last spot in Elf Land that still has dens and plants. If he digs in Drum Hill, where will we go?"

"King Gris will bring the end of Elf

Land if we do not stop him!" Twigs is
sad. "So Matt and Liz, you must help
us!"

Chapter 5

The Spelling Pen

"I still do not get what we can do to help," Matt says.

"The Spelling Pen!" say Mell and Twigs.

"This?" Matt has his pen in his hand. "What can this pen do to help?"

"It can do a lot!" says Twigs. "It will stop King Gris and fix this land."

"Yes," nods Mell. "With the Spelling Pen, we have a shot at winning. Tell us what spells you do in your land with the Spelling Pen. Then we can get a plan."

"Matt just got this pen as a gift from Grandma Deb. It has no spells!" says Liz.

"Pens are to jot down with. We do not cast spells with them."

"I think there is a mix up. When we say spell, it is spelling as in A-B-C. Not the spell you cast. Got it?" Matt says.

"But the pen got you to Elf Land," Twigs says. "Did it not? So it can do spells. What did you do for the pen to bring you to Elf Land?"

"Well, I was just jotting on a pad," Matt says. "I had a wish to vanish."

"You did vanish from your land," Mell says. "The pen will cast a spell if you can jot it down."

"I get it," Liz says. "I can spell well. Let me test the pen!"

She grabs the pen from Matt. She jots on her hand, "I wish... for a big dish of fish!"

But not a thing. No big fish or a dish.

"Why was there no spell?" Liz asks.

She hands the pen to Mell. He spins it to check it out. It is intact.

"Is this your pen or Matt's?" Twigs asks.

"It was a gift to Matt," Liz says.

"That is it. The pen is his, so it is just Matt who can do the spelling. It is Matt that can help Elf Land."

"Then Elf Land is in a big jam," Liz says.

"Why do you say that?" Mell and Twigs ask.

Matt is glum.

"My penmanship is bad and I cannot spell well," he says. "And I panic!"

"Matt, just think of this... If you see it, you can have it. If you see it, you will get it." Mell taps Matt on the chest with the pen. "Just trust your instinct."

"You must not panic," Twigs adds. "If you panic, there will be no spell."

Just then, there is a big crash. And lots of yells.

Chapter 6

A Mad Goblin

An elf in pink runs into the hut.

"Mell! Twigs!" she says. "A goblin is on its way to the huts. Can the Sun Kids stop him?"

Twigs and Mell jump up. "Matt!" Twigs says, "You must stop the goblin with the Spelling Pen. Help us!"

"But what can I do?" Matt asks.

"Jot with the pen!" says Twigs. Then he grabs Matt's hand and they run out of the hut. "We must stop the goblin fast! If he gets past us, he will stomp the huts and munch up all our stuff."

"Do the goblins do that a lot?" Matt asks.

"In the past, they did not," Twigs says. "But King Gris has cut the plants. So goblins have to rob us to get nuts and plants."

Matt, Liz, Twigs and Mell go out. They run down the path.

There is a lot of crashing and bashing.

A big goblin is in the path. He is as big as an elk and has a vast gut.

He swings his club and yells, "Get out of my way! Or I will smash you into dust!"

The elf clan stands on the path in front of the goblin.

"We will not let you pass," says Mell to the goblin. "You cannot get to the huts."

The goblin gets mad. He yells back and hits a branch. The branch splits into bits.

"Stop!" Twigs yells. "You cannot get in. The Sun Kids and the Spelling Pen will stop you!"

Matt wants to run. But he cannot. It is as if his legs are stuck in a rock.

The goblin spots Matt next to Twigs.

"A kid?" he sniffs. "So what?" he cracks up.

He grips his club. "Sun Kid or not, I will get my lunch!" he says.

"Matt! Do a spell! Quick!" yells Mell.

But Matt just stands still. "What can I do?" he thinks.

The goblin swings his club.

Liz grabs the pen from Matt and runs in front of the elf clan.

"Stop, bad goblin!" she yells.

Chapter 7

The Pact

Matt and the elf clan stand in shock as small Liz sprints in front of the big goblin.

"I tell you to stop!" She lifts the pen and wags it at the goblin.

There is no spell. But the goblin stops. He has to bend to spot Liz.

"This is the Spelling Pen and we are the Sun Kids," she blasts.

"I am not a bad goblin. I just want a bit of lunch. That is all!" he begs.

This big goblin may not be as bad as Liz thinks.

"I am Hull," he tells Liz. "My Gran has told me of the Sun Kids and the things they can do to bad goblins. But I am not a bad goblin. Not at all," he insists. "There are no nuts or bugs left in Ash Hill. I am so peckish! What must a goblin do to be fed?"

Matt steps up next to Liz.

"What do you think?" Liz asks Matt.

"If I do not smash the huts, can I still have lunch?" Hull begs.

"Well, yes!" Matt says. "Are there fish in the ponds?" he asks Mell.

"Yes," Mell says. "We can still get fish in most spots."

"Do not smash the huts. Go and fish.

That can be your lunch," Matt tells Hull. He pats the goblin's back.

"Thanks," Hull grins. "And just to check... The Sun Kids will not punish me. Yes?"

"Yes," nods Twigs. "I will tell you where the best spot to fish is. Let me grab rods for us and I will go with you. I will fish for lunch as well." He runs to the hut to get the rods.

Hull sits on a rock.

"I wish things were not this way," says Hull. "Will you fix things in Elf Land? Can you bring us back to the old days of bliss?" he asks Matt and Liz.

The kids can tell they can trust Hull.

"It is a big task," says Matt.

"Yes, it is," admits Hull. "King Gris limits all the plants we can get. I cannot tell what the imps want. But I can tell you that the goblins do not want King Gris. We help him just to get a bit to snack on."

"So why do you not stop him?" asks Liz.

"But how?" asks Hull. "We are stuck with him. You are the Sun Kids. Can you bring an end to King Gris? "

"Yes," Mell jumps in the chat. "The Sun Kids plan to fix this mess."

"We will do what we can," Matt cuts Mell off. "With help from the elf clan."

He does not have a hint of how
to fix this mess. He does not want to
crush Hull's trust.

Hull sits and rubs his chin.

Then he slaps his club in his hand and
says, "With help from the elf clan and
me. I will help you stop King Gris. It is
a pact!"

Chapter 8

The Plan

Matt, Liz and Mell are in shock.

"You want to help us?" Mell asks Hull.

"Yes," Hull says. "I am sad that the goblins must pinch plants from the elf clan. I am sad that the griffins have left. King Gris will not quit. We must stop him. We must bring Elf Land back to how it was."

"What do the Sun Kids think?" Mell asks.

"I think that we must get all the help we can," Matt says.

"Hull is big and strong. He will be a big help," says Liz.

"O.K.," says Mell. "We will let you help! Thanks, Hull."

"But I must get lunch. Did you say there are lots of fish in the pond?" Hull grins.

Twigs is back from the hut with rods and a big bucket.

"Let us go get fish," Twigs says to Hull. "We will fill this bucket to the rim with fish."

Mell says, "Hull wants to help stop King Gris."

"No kidding." This stuns Twigs.

Hull taps his chin with a grin. "Let us fish, then plan."

Twigs picks up the bucket. Hull grabs the rods. They go on the path to the pond.

"Let us go back to my hut to think of a plan," Mell says.

The kids go with Mell. As they go, Liz tells Matt, "I am so glad that Hull will help. He is not a bad goblin."

Matt nods. "Not at all."

In the hut, the kids sit as Mell brings them drinks and lunch.

"What is your plan?' Liz asks as they munch. "What will you do?"

The elf clan and Hull think that Matt can stop King Gris. But Matt cannot think how he can do it.

"I must think," Matt says. "We must all think."

Matt sips his drink. Then he jumps up. He has a plan.

"I bet, it is not just Hull that wants to stop King Gris. We may get a bunch of goblins that want to stop him as well."

Liz jumps up as well. "That is terrific. I bet his goblin pals are just as big. They will be a big help,"

Mell slams down his mug. "That is it. We have got to be in a big pact with the goblins to kick King Gris out of Elf Land."

Chapter 9

No Way Out

As Mell, Matt and Liz discuss the plan, Twigs and Hull are back from the pond with lots of fish.

Hull is big and cannot fit in the hut. So the kids and Mell go out. They all sit in front of the hut. Mell grills the fish in a pan.

Hull is glad to get fresh fish. He gulps down his lunch and licks the dish. Then, he sets his dish on the grass.

"Yum!" Hull thanks as he rubs his big gut.

Mell nods with a grin.

"What is the plan?" Hull asks. "How can we stop King Gris?"

"We will get to that," Matt says. "But I want to ask... Do you think the rest of the goblins will want to help us?"

Hull nods. "I bet they will," he says. "Goblins are sick of all this rot. We want things back to when all of Elf Land was glad."

"This will be grand!" says Liz. "The goblins, the elf clan and the Sun Kids will stop King Gris."

"Where is the king?" asks Matt.

"His camp is at Ash Hill," Mell says.

"It is just next to where we are!" says Twigs.

"It will not be long until he will finish his dig at Ash Hill. Then his next big gold dig will be at Drum Hill," adds Mell. "We are at so much risk as well."

"Not Drum Hill," Hull gasps. "We are at Drum Hill. This is the best of Elf Land!"

"Yes," says Twigs. "It is the last bit he has not dug up yet."

"Tell you what," Hull says as he jumps up. "Mell. Twigs. Let us run down to the goblin dens. They are just down the path. We can tell them the plan. We can bring all the goblins to the Sun Kids."

But Twigs says, "I think we must not go to the dens with you. Ask the goblins if they want to help. If they say yes, bring them back with you."

"Got it!" Hull nods. He gets his big club and stamps off.

Mell says to Twigs, "Let us go and tell the rest of the elf clan what we plan to do."

"Yes, we must," Twigs says.

Matt thinks this big pact may dismiss him and the Spelling Pen. They may not want him to cast a spell.

But then Twigs adds, "Kids, do not forget the Spelling Pen. You must have it with you to help Elf Land."

Chapter 10

Help From The Goblins

"Matt, you get the Spelling Pen," Liz says when it is just them left in front of the hut.

They go back in the hut. Matt is glum. "This is mad!" he snaps.

"What is up with you?" Liz does not get why Matt is upset.

Matt picks up the pen and spins it in his hand.

"It is just us in the hut," Liz tells Matt. "Test the pen when you can."

Matt gets a pad to jot on. But he stalls. "What do I do?"

"Think of a wish and jot it on the pad," Liz says. "And do not forget to trust your gut!"

Matt grips the pen.

He thinks and thinks.

"But it must be a wish that I can spell! What I can spell will not help stop King Gris!"

He flings the pen onto the pad.

Liz begs him to test the pen but he will not pick it up.

Just then, there are lots of thudding steps. The kids jump up. Matt picks up the pen fast. They run out of the hut.

The elf clan drops what they do and

sprint to the path to check what the thuds are. They all gasp.

A big gang of goblins stomps on the path. Hull is in front.

An elf kid says, "Will the goblins rob us?"

"Shush," says the elf mom. "The goblins want to help."

Hull brings the goblins up to the huts.

"Just like the elf clan, we want an end to King Gris's big digs," Hull says.

"It is a pact," Twigs says. "We are so glad! Then we must set off for Ash Hill."

The elf clan, the goblins and the kids clap.

Hull tells the goblins, "These are the kids I told you of."

"Ah!" say the goblins. "The Sun Kids!"

A big goblin in black says to Matt, "Hull says you have the Spelling Pen. Is that so?"

Matt nods. He lifts up the Spelling Pen.

The goblins gasp.

"Then the Sun Kid will stop King Gris!" A goblin yells.

The goblin next to him says, "Just tell us what to do to help. We will do all we can."

"Thanks," Matt says. "But I think Twigs will tell us when to go and what to do."

"We will set off at sunset. We will crash the king's camp!" Twigs says. "Then Matt will tell us what to do."

Chapter 11

The Trip to Ash Hill

The sun sets and it gets dim. The goblins thump their clubs. Matt checks that the Spelling Pen is in his pocket.

"Are the Sun Kids set to go?" Mell asks.

Matt and Liz nod.

"And the Spelling Pen?" Mell adds.

Matt taps his pocket.

The elf clan and the goblins are set as well. They all stomp off on the path. As they go, the goblins thump their big clubs and chant:

The king has plans to dig and dig

To slash up all the plants and twigs.

But with a stamp and tramp and hop

We go, we go to set a stop.

Goblins, elf clan hand in hand

To fix the mess in our Elf Land.

The Sun Kids and the Pen that spells

Will stop the king, this we can tell.

Liz claps her hands and chants with the goblins. The elf clan chants as well.

But Matt does not chant. He is not glad to be a Sun Kid. He is not glad to have the Spelling Pen. This is all so much for him.

"They expect me to stop King Gris with this pen. But I cannot!" he thinks. He just wants to slip back into his shell. "This is all fun for Liz. But she just does not get it!"

As they get to Ash Hill, the plants thin out. There are big gaps from a plant to the next. Then, the plants vanish. The land on the hill is full of pits and cracks.

Matt thinks they must be at Ash Hill. This must be where King Gris's camp is.

The chants stop. They stand still. It is a grim plot of land. This is what Elf Land will be if the king does not quit his digs. They are all sad.

They all stop when they get to the hill.

"This is Ash Hill!" Hull says. "Or what is left of it. Elf Land must not end as a big pit with no plants and no spirit. This is why we must stop King Gris!"

"Stop the king! Stop the king!" the goblins yell. They thump their clubs.

Just then, a gust of wind runs down the hill. A thick fog rests on Ash Hill like a blanket. The swish of wings fills the fog. Matt spots lots of things with big wings. The things rush to them from the hill top.

Chapter 12

The Imps and The Duchess

"Are they bats?" yelps Matt.

"Imps!" yell the elf clan and goblins. "Lots and lots of them!"

"Imps?" says Liz. "I do not think they are in our pact!"

"No," says Twigs. He stands next to Liz. "They help King Gris."

Matt and Liz flinch. This is a big bunch of imps. The pack is led by an imp with big black wings. She lands with a thump.

The rest of the imps land in front and back of the goblins and the elf clan. They block the path for them. The elf clan, the goblins and the kids are in a big pinch.

The big imp says, "Your chants say stop the king? Who is this mob that wants to stop King Gris? What on..."

"We will stop him," Hull cuts off the big imp. He must not dig out or slash the plants."

"Who says the king must stop?" asks the big imp.

The imps hiss.

"The elf clan and the goblins!" says Mell. "We have the Sun Kids to help us. They have the Spelling Pen!"

"Is that a fact?" The big imp spots Matt and Liz. "I must tell the king that

I, the Duchess of Imps, got the Sun Kids. And the Spelling Pen. Grab them all, imps!" she yells.

"Quick, Matt!" Twigs yells. "Cast a spell with the pen!"

The imps stop for a bit in shock. They do not want spells cast on them.

Matt's hand is stiff.

"I cannot! I just cannot do it!" he sobs.

"Ha ha!" says the Duchess. "Is this the Sun Kid you had your trust in? Well then, we are in luck. Get them, imps!"

The imps grab the kids and the elf clan. The goblins pick up their clubs to swing. But the imps are fast. They get a quick grip on the goblins as well.

"To the King's Den!" yells the Duchess.

Chapter 13

The King's Den

With big flaps of their wings, the imps lift off.

Matt swings at the grip of an imp. Its big wings flap and they rush in the wind.

The imps land on top of the hill. They are in front of a big den dug into the black rock.

"Go and call for King Gris," the big imp says. "Tell him the Duchess of Imps has a gift for him."

Matt is so sad. He has let them all down. And now they are all in the hands of King Gris.

"I am such a flop," sobs Matt. "I had a shot to help. But I did not do a thing. I am no Sun Kid."

"It is O.K.," Twigs says. "It is not the end yet."

"All the goblins still trust you, Matt," adds Hull.

"You do?" asks Matt in shock.

"We as well," says Twigs.

Liz grabs his hand. "Just trust your gut! You can do this!"

Just then, an elf exits the den. He is gruff and fat. He has pinkish skin. His top and pants are of rich, red silk. Lots of gold rings are on his hands and he has gold strings hanging from his neck.

This must be the king.

He steps in front of the imps.

"Ha ha!" the elf claps. "I am the King of Elf Land."

"Ha ha!" the imps mimic the King. "He is the King of Elf Land."

"The elf clan, the goblins and the Sun Kids," King Gris sniffs. "There is a plot to kick me out, eh? And this is the bunch that will stop me? What a big flop!" he blasts.

Liz and Matt can tell King Gris is a pest.

"If I stack you all up, you do not sum up to my skills," the king mocks them. "I will punish you all. You will have to dig in my pits and get me lots of gold."

Liz steps up. Her hands are in fists and she is mad. "You, King Gris, are a bad king," she yells.

"Liz, shut up!" says Matt as he tugs at Liz's hand.

"I will not," says Liz. "I will tell this bad king just what I think of him."

Chapter 14

The Shift

"What?" says King Gris.

This is a big shock. He has not had a kid stand up to him.

"I tell you. You are a bad king. All you want is gold, gold, gold. And as you dig for it, you trash Elf Land. Can you not think?" Liz rants.

The king snaps at the Imp Duchess. "Stop that brat! Grab her! Dump them all in the pits."

Matt steps in front of Liz and says, "You imps can do what King Gris says. You can lock us up. But you will be sad if the king does not stop. When he kills

Elf Land, what will the imps do? I do not think the king will let you get your hands on his gold. And if he does, will you munch on gold?"

They all gasp and stand still in shock as Matt blasts.

"You smash the plants and kill the land for all," Matt adds. "Check out what your digs did to this land. The griffins have left. The plants are lost. Elf Land is grim. You will get a big stack of gold to sit on top of a grim land. You will have to snack on your gold for that is all that will be left!"

The imps stop and check what the Imp Duchess will say.

King Gris is so mad that he cannot say a thing. He is red hot mad.

Mell steps up and yells, "We can tell this will not end well unless the king stops. Stick with us, the Duchess of the Imps. Elf Land is not just for you. Or the goblins or the elf clan. It is for all of us. If the king kills our land, it will be the end for all of us."

"Do not stop!" yells King Gris to the imps. "Grab them! Drop them all into the pits!"

But the imps are not so quick to do what the king says.

"Duchess?" asks an imp. "What must we do?"

The Imp Duchess stands still and thinks.

"You imps can do what is just,"

Matt says. "Help the elf clan and the goblins win back Elf Land!"

King Gris stamps and yells. "No! Shut that kid up!"

"Imps! Help us!" Matt insists.

"Imps! The kids, the goblins and the elf clan have the best intent," the Duchess says. "This king has led us to do bad things," she adds. "He will kill our land. We must bring an end to this mess. We must stop him. Grab the king!"

The king slinks to the back of the Duchess. He plans to run off down the hill. He wants to get out of Ash Hill as fast as he can.

Matt grabs the Spelling Pen and the pad. He thinks of the elf clan and goblins. He thinks of how Elf Land will end up if he cannot stop the king.

"If I see it, I can have it. If I see it, I will get it," he hums.

Chapter 15
Matt's Spell

Matt does not stop to think that he cannot spell.

He squints.

He does not want the king to run. And as quick as a flash, he jots:

"S-T-O-P. STOP."

Then he drafts a sketch of his wish: The imps, the elf clan, the goblins, all help ban King Gris from the land.

The pen glints. Then there is a big flash from the pen.

The imps all blink at the flash and gasp.

The king's red silk outfit glints just like the pen. When he lifts his leg for his next step, he is stuck. He cannot run off.

A big imp jumps on the king and grabs him.

The Duchess lets her big wings out. "The goblins, the elf clan and the Sun Kids are our pals. Lock up the king in his den. We will think of what to do with him."

The goblins and the elf clan chant with a thrill.

Liz claps her hands.

"You did it, Matt!" she says. "You did cast a spell with the pen!"

Mell, Twigs and Hull pat Matt on the back. All the rest yell and clap their hands as well.

Hull says, "What a glad day for Elf Land! What a win!"

"I say we got our land back from the king," says the Duchess.

Yet, she is sad.

"The king will not dig. But the plants are still lost. There are no buds to bring them back," she says.

Her chin drops to her chest.

"The king did all this with help from us. This is what the imps did to Elf Land."

"I think I can help fix that!" Matt says. He lifts the pen up. "Fill up the pits. Fix Elf Land. Bring back the plants," he hums.

Then he maps an Elf Land on the pad. He fills it with lots of plants, sun and bliss.

Just like that, the land enchants. A mist masks the rocks.

As all stand in shock, the grass springs up. In a quick flash, they all stand on fresh wet grass, not on grim black rocks.

Lots and lots of big and small shrubs fill up Ash Hill, then the rest of the land. Bugs rest on buds.

The Spelling Pen still glints in Matt's hand. This is just what he did think of. This is just what he felt Elf land must be like.

All the goblins, the imps and the elf clan gasp and chant in bliss. "You did it, Matt! You did it!"

"You are the best!" Liz yells.

"Thanks," Matt says. "But we all did it."

Chapter 16

Back from Elf Land

The sun is up. This is a fresh day for Elf Land.

The trip back to Drum Hill is fun on a day like this. The goblins, the elf clan and the imps sing and chant. They plan a big fest for all.

At the fest, Matt asks the Duchess if they will ban the king from Elf Land.

"We will let King Gris dig," she grins. "But not for gold pits. He will dig in a ranch for crops."

Matt grins back.

Liz sits next to Matt. "How did you

jot all that so fast with the Spelling Pen?" she asks.

Matt winks at Liz. "I just did what I had to do. Mell had the best tip for me: If I see it, I will have it. If I see it, I will get it. So that is just what I did. When I did not panic, it all went well. Plus, it was not just a script, but a sketch as well."

"A sketch?" Liz did not think of that. "You impress me, Matt."

"Best of all, I get that we all have distinct skills. There are a lot of ways to do a task. And setbacks do not have to be a bad thing. They can in fact help. So I just do my best," Matt lifts his fist up.

"This is the Sun Kid Matt."

"And that gets me to think that we must go back. It was fun in Elf Land, but we must go back to our land," he adds.

"Yes, we must," Liz says. "I miss Mom and Dad."

"I miss them as well," says Matt. "Our quest in Elf Land ends. But we may still be back to Elf Land to visit them."

"Plus, I do not think this is the last quest for the Spelling Pen," Liz winks at Matt.

The goblins and imps are still at the fest. The kids slip off the path. The elf clan does not see them go.

Liz grabs Matt's hand. He picks up the pad and jots down with the Spelling Pen: "I wish to go back to Mom and Dad."

With a big flash and a quick spin, Elf Land and all vanish.

Matt and Liz land with a thump on Matt's bed. At last, they are back.

"Yes, we did it. We are back," they jump on the bed.

Their mom is in the hall. "Matt, did you finish it yet?" she asks.

"In just a sec, Mom!" Matt calls down the steps.

"With such a big win on this quest, spelling will not panic me," Matt winks at Liz. "I think it will all be O.K. in class as well."

Then Matt spots the trash bin. The tag with the sun that was on the pen is still in the bin. He gets the tag. He tucks the Spelling Pen in his desk and sets the tag next to it. Then he picks up a fresh pen from his bag.

"What will you do with that pen?" asks Liz, as Matt has it in his hand.

"I will finish the script to Grandma. But I will not print it. It must be with a pen," he grins.

Matt jots:

"Quests bring out the sun in us and melt the rocks that block our path.

Thanks to your gift, at last, not a thing stands in my way on this day.

I cannot express how much I cherish this pen. It is the best gift.

Thanks for the pen, Grandma Deb.

XOXO

Your Grandson,

Sun Kid Matt."

You can download full color

CERTIFICATE OF ACCOMPLISHMENT

and

CERTIFICATE OF COMPLETION

On our website

SIMPLEWORDSBOOKS.COM

Certificate of Accomplishment

This certificate is awarded to

_____

for successful completion of

Spelling Pen   in Elf Land

_____
Signature

_____
Date

SIMPLE
WORDS

SPELLING PEN
IN ELF LAND
WORD LIST

#	Word	Count	#	Word	Count	#	Word	Count
1	a	171	26	best	13	51	bunch	4
2	adds	12	27	bet	3	52	but	53
3	admits	1	28	big	64	53	by	2
4	ahh	1	29	bin	3	54	call	2
5	all	64	30	bit	6	55	calls	2
6	am	14	31	bits	1	56	camp	3
7	an	16	32	black	8	57	can	58
8	and	168	33	blanket	1	58	cannot	20
9	are	73	34	blast	2	59	cap	2
10	as	53	35	blasts	3	60	cast	7
11	ash	11	36	blink	1	61	chant	5
12	ask	4	37	bliss	4	62	chants	4
13	asks	35	38	block	2	63	chat	1
14	at	29	39	blocks	6	64	check	7
15	back	31	40	box	6	65	checks	2
16	bad	17	41	branch	2	66	cherish	1
17	bag	2	42	brat	1	67	chest	2
18	ban	2	43	bring	12	68	chin	3
19	bashing	1	44	brings	4	69	clan	36
20	bats	1	45	brink	1	70	clap	2
21	be	34	46	brunch	2	71	claps	3
22	bed	4	47	bucket	3	72	class	2
23	begs	3	48	buds	2	73	club	5
24	bench	2	49	bug	1	74	clubs	4
25	bend	1	50	bugs	2	75	cost	1

#	Word	Count	#	Word	Count	#	Word	Count
76	cracks	2	101	do	68	126	express	1
77	cram	1	102	does	21	127	fact	2
78	crash	2	103	down	20	128	fast	7
79	crashing	1	104	drafts	1	129	fat	1
80	crops	1	105	drink	4	130	fed	1
81	crush	1	106	drinks	2	131	felt	1
82	cup	1	107	drips	1	132	fest	3
83	cut	2	108	drop	4	133	fill	4
84	cuts	2	109	drops	3	134	fills	4
85	dad	6	110	drum	6	135	finish	5
86	day	6	111	duchess	14	136	fish	14
87	days	1	112	dug	5	137	fist	1
88	deb	8	113	dull	1	138	fists	1
89	den	6	114	dump	1	139	fit	1
90	dens	3	115	dust	1	140	fix	7
91	desk	4	116	eggs	2	141	flap	1
92	did	31	117	eh	1	142	flaps	1
93	dig	12	118	elf	93	143	flash	7
94	digs	4	119	elk	1	144	flinch	1
95	dim	2	120	emits	1	145	flings	2
96	dips	1	121	enchants	1	146	flop	2
97	discuss	1	122	end	9	147	fog	3
98	dish	6	123	ends	1	148	fond	1
99	dismiss	1	124	exits	1	149	for	42
100	distinct	1	125	expect	1	150	forget	2

#	Word	Count		#	Word	Count		#	Word	Count
151	forgets	1		176	gold	15		201	hall	2
152	fresh	4		177	got	12		202	ham	2
153	from	25		178	grab	7		203	hand	18
154	front	12		179	grabs	10		204	hands	10
155	full	1		180	gran	1		205	hanging	1
156	fun	4		181	grand	2		206	has	19
157	fuss	1		182	grandma	9		207	have	27
158	gang	2		183	grandson	1		208	he	160
159	gaps	1		184	grass	4		209	help	36
160	gasp	5		185	griffin	1		210	helps	2
161	gasps	4		186	griffins	10		211	her	14
162	get	48		187	grills	1		212	hill	23
163	gets	14		188	grim	4		213	him	22
164	getting	1		189	grin	2		214	hint	1
165	gift	12		190	grins	7		215	his	64
166	gifts	7		191	grip	2		216	hiss	1
167	glad	11		192	grips	2		217	hits	1
168	glass	2		193	Gris	35		218	hop	1
169	glint	1		194	gruff	1		219	hot	2
170	glinting	1		195	grunts	2		220	how	10
171	glints	5		196	gulps	2		221	hugs	2
172	glum	2		197	gust	1		222	Hull	42
173	go	32		198	gut	4		223	hums	2
174	goblin	25		199	ha	6		224	hut	13
175	goblins	49		200	had	6		225	huts	8

#	Word	Count	#	Word	Count	#	Word	Count
226	I	114	251	kept	1	276	lists	1
227	if	24	252	kick	2	277	Liz	90
228	imp	12	253	kid	16	278	lock	2
229	impress	1	254	kidding	1	279	log	1
230	imps	37	255	kids	49	280	long	2
231	in	112	256	kill	3	281	lost	3
232	ink	7	257	kills	2	282	lot	6
233	insists	4	258	kiln	1	283	lots	14
234	instinct	1	259	king	73	284	luck	2
235	intact	1	260	land	70	285	lunch	8
236	intent	1	261	lands	1	286	mad	5
237	into	11	262	last	11	287	maps	1
238	i-pad	1	263	led	2	288	masks	1
239	is	155	264	left	12	289	Matt	171
240	it	103	265	leg	1	290	may	5
241	its	2	266	legs	1	291	me	18
242	jam	1	267	let	14	292	Mell	45
243	jet	1	268	lets	1	293	melt	2
244	jobs	1	269	licks	1	294	mess	5
245	jot	7	270	lift	1	295	milk	1
246	jots	5	271	lifts	5	296	mimic	1
247	jotting	1	272	like	12	297	miss	3
248	jump	3	273	likes	1	298	mist	1
249	jumps	7	274	limits	1	299	mix	2
250	just	50	275	list	3	300	mob	1

#	Word	Count	#	Word	Count	#	Word	Count
301	mocks	1	326	or	15	351	pinkish	1
302	mom	16	327	our	14	352	pit	1
303	most	3	328	out	21	353	pits	6
304	much	3	329	outfit	2	354	plan	16
305	mug	2	330	pack	1	355	plans	2
306	munch	3	331	pact	5	356	plant	1
307	must	42	332	pad	8	357	plants	18
308	my	12	333	pals	2	358	play	4
309	neck	1	334	pan	2	359	plot	2
310	next	15	335	panic	6	360	plum	1
311	no	24	336	pants	2	361	plums	1
312	nod	1	337	pass	1	362	plus	5
313	nods	10	338	past	5	363	pocket	5
314	not	97	339	pat	1	364	pond	3
315	now	1	340	path	17	365	ponds	1
316	nuts	2	341	pats	1	366	pot	2
317	O.K.	5	342	peckish	1	367	print	1
318	obelisk	1	343	pen	83	368	punish	2
319	odd	2	344	penmanship	2	369	quest	5
320	of	110	345	pens	2	370	quests	1
321	off	13	346	pest	1	371	quick	10
322	oh	1	347	pick	3	372	quit	2
323	old	2	348	picks	7	373	rabbits	1
324	on	51	349	pinch	3	374	ranch	1
325	onto	1	350	pink	1	375	rants	1

#	Word	Count
376	red	6
377	rest	9
378	rests	2
379	rich	3
380	rim	1
381	ring	1
382	rings	1
383	rips	3
384	risk	2
385	rob	2
386	rock	4
387	rocks	3
388	rods	4
389	rot	1
390	rubs	2
391	rug	1
392	run	12
393	runs	9
394	rush	3
395	rushing	1
396	sad	9
397	say	12
398	says	111
399	script	2
400	sec	2

#	Word	Count
401	see	7
402	selfish	1
403	send	1
404	set	7
405	setbacks	1
406	sets	5
407	shall	2
408	she	38
409	shell	1
410	shh	1
411	shock	9
412	shot	2
413	shrubs	1
414	shush	2
415	shut	2
416	siblings	1
417	sick	1
418	silk	2
419	sing	1
420	sings	1
421	sink	1
422	sips	2
423	sit	5
424	sits	4
425	six	2

#	Word	Count
426	sketch	3
427	skills	2
428	skin	1
429	slams	1
430	slaps	1
431	slash	2
432	slinks	1
433	slip	2
434	slips	1
435	slug	1
436	small	3
437	smash	4
438	smell	1
439	smug	1
440	snack	3
441	snaps	2
442	sniffs	2
443	so	26
444	sobbing	1
445	sobs	2
446	son	2
447	spell	18
448	spelling	32
449	spells	6
450	spend	1

#	Word	Count	#	Word	Count	#	Word	Count
451	spin	4	476	stomps	1	501	test	3
452	spinning	1	477	stop	43	502	thank	2
453	spins	2	478	stops	5	503	thanks	9
454	spirit	1	479	string	1	504	that	59
455	splits	1	480	strings	1	505	the	477
456	spot	5	481	strong	1	506	their	9
457	spots	7	482	stuck	3	507	them	28
458	springs	2	483	stuff	1	508	then	39
459	sprint	1	484	stuns	1	509	there	24
460	sprints	1	485	such	2	510	these	1
461	squints	1	486	sum	1	511	they	62
462	stack	4	487	sun	43	512	thick	2
463	stalls	1	488	sunset	1	513	thicket	3
464	stamp	1	489	swing	2	514	thin	1
465	stamps	2	490	swings	3	515	thing	8
466	stand	7	491	swish	1	516	things	10
467	stands	8	492	tag	6	517	think	35
468	step	1	493	tall	2	518	thinks	17
469	steps	15	494	tank	6	519	this	68
470	stick	1	495	taps	3	520	thrill	2
471	sticking	1	496	task	2	521	thud	1
472	sticks	2	497	tell	25	522	thudding	2
473	stiff	1	498	tells	6	523	thuds	1
474	still	17	499	ten	1	524	thump	5
475	stomp	2	500	terrific	1	525	tip	1

#	Word	Count
526	to	163
527	told	3
528	top	6
529	tramp	1
530	trash	3
531	trip	1
532	trust	7
533	tucks	1
534	tugs	1
535	Twigs	51
536	unless	1
537	unpacks	1
538	until	3
539	up	51
540	upset	2
541	us	35
542	vanish	5
543	vast	1
544	visit	1
545	wags	1
546	wall	3
547	walls	1
548	want	20
549	wants	9
550	was	19

#	Word	Count
551	way	4
552	ways	1
553	we	81
554	well	29
555	went	2
556	were	2
557	west	1
558	wet	1
559	what	61
560	when	12
561	where	12
562	who	7
563	why	8
564	will	84
565	win	4
566	wind	2
567	wings	6
568	winks	3
569	winning	1
570	wish	13
571	with	64
572	XOXO	1
573	yell	4
574	yells	22
575	yelps	1

#	Word	Count
576	yes	19
577	yet	10
578	you	108
579	your	21
580	yum	3
Total Words		**7096**

Do you want to write your own story now?

Written by: _____

_____

_____

_____

_____

_____

_____

_____

_____

_____

_____

_____

_____

_____

_____

_____

_____

_____

_____

_____

_____

_____

_____

Do you want to draw your own story now?

Illustrated by:

WANT TO READ MORE
CHAPTER BOOKS

Spelling Pen
Red Obelisk

by C. Knebel

FOX HUNT

by Cigdem Knebel

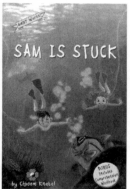

SAM IS STUCK

by Cigdem Knebel

The Gold of
Black Rock Hill

by C. Knebel

Six Days at Camp
With Jack and Max

by Cigdem Knebel

Six Days at Camp
With Lin and Jill

by Cigdem Knebel

*STUDY
GUIDES*

FOX HUNT
Comprehension Workbook

by Cigdem Knebel

Spelling Pen
Red Obelisk

Comprehension
Workbook

by C.Knebel

Spelling Pen in Elf Land
Comprehension Workbook

by C.Knebel

SAM IS STUCK
Comprehension Workbook

by Cigdem Knebel

SAM IS STUCK
Phonics Workbook

by Cigdem Knebel

Six Days at Camp
Comprehension Workbook

With Jack
and Max

by Cigdem Knebel

VISIT OUR WEBSITE FOR FREE RESOURCES

simplewordsbooks.com

AND CHECK OUT OUR FREE ONLINE SUMMITS

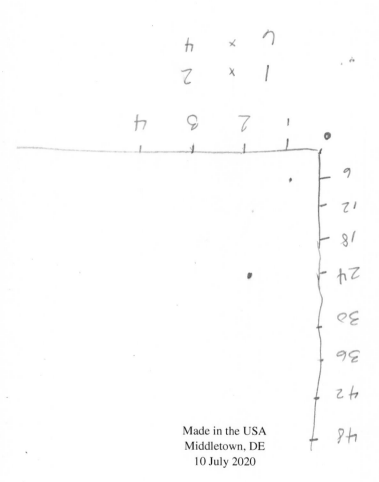